JEREMY ISN'T HUNGRY
by Barbara Williams
pictures by Martha Alexander

E. P. Dutton · New York

Library of Congress Cataloging in Publication Data

Williams, Barbara.   Jeremy isn't hungry.
SUMMARY: A youngster's attempts to amuse and feed
his baby brother almost end in disaster.
[1. Brothers and sisters—Fiction]   I. Alexander,
Martha G.   II. Title.
PZ7.W65587Je 1978   [E]   78-4924   ISBN: 0-525-32760-6

Published in the United States by E.P. Dutton, a Division
of Sequoia-Elsevier Publishing Company, Inc., New York

Published simultaneously in Canada by Clarke,
Irwin & Company Limited, Toronto and Vancouver

Editor: Ann Durell   Designer: Riki Levinson
Printed in the U.S.A.   First Edition
10 9 8 7 6 5 4 3 2 1

For Gloria Skurzynski
B.W.

For Anne
M.A.

"Mama, Jeremy doesn't want me to tend him anymore. He's crying for *you*....Mama?...Mama?... Can you hear me, Mama?"

"Were you calling me, Davey?"

"Yes, Mama. Jeremy's crying."

"I can't come now, Davey. I'm hurrying to get ready for your sister's program at school."

"Jeremy's crying hard."

"He's probably hungry, Davey. Put him in his table-chair, and you can start feeding him until the baby-sitter comes."

"Come on, Jeremy boy. Ups-a-baby. Stop kicking, you little dope. Mama, he won't let me carry him. He wants *you*."

"I can't come right now, Davey. Smile at him and make him think you're playing a game."

"Ho, ho, ho! I'm jolly old Saint Nicholas, and you're my bag of toys. Isn't this fun?... Come on, Jeremy, *bend*. What do you think you are? A bag of icicles? *Mama, Jeremy won't let me bend him!*"

"DON'T BEND HIM, DAVEY!
I'M COMING RIGHT NOW! I'M COMING....
OUCH!"

"You have soap bubbles on your feet, Mama.
You'll fall down if you run with soap bubbles
on your feet."

"Yes, Davey."

"Come on, Jeremy, sit in your table-chair
and be a good boy. Get a jar of baby food from
the pantry, Davey. Remember to smile and
make him think you're playing a game."

"Well, well, Jeremy boy. I'm Mr. Dudley,
the supermarket man. What kind of food do you
want today? Look at me, Jeremy. I'm smiling."

"Mama, Jeremy doesn't care that I'm smiling."

"Were you calling me, Davey?"
"What kind of baby food does Jeremy like?"
"Give him beef soup. He likes beef soup."

"Okay. Mama?"
"Yes, Davey?"
"How do I tell which one is beef soup?"
"It says *beef soup* on the label."
"Okay."

"Mama?"

"Yes, Davey?"

"I can't read."

"Oh, I forgot. Beef soup is the brown one that looks nasty."

"There aren't any brown ones. How about an orange one that looks nasty?"

"Orange? Oh, you mean carrots. Yes, he likes carrots. Sometimes."

"Today he doesn't like carrots, Mama."
"Try heating them."
"Okay."

"Mama?"

"Yes, Davey?"

"I don't know how to heat carrots."

"Just put a little hot water in a pan and set the jar of baby food in it until it gets warm."

"I don't know how to turn on the stove, Mama."

"DON'T TOUCH THE STOVE, DAVEY! I'M COMING!"

"See, you just use hot water from the tap.
Understand?"

"Yes, Mama."

"Any more questions?"

"Yes, Mama. Are you going to wear your hair like that to school?"

"Not if you'll be a good boy and feed the baby."

"Okay."

"Be quiet, Jeremy. I'm heating your carrots, la-lah. There. Don't they look good? Yuck! They sure don't smell very good. Open your mouth, Jeremy. Darn it!... Look, Jeremy. Here's a choo-choo train coming up the track to the tunnel. Choo-choo-choo-choo. Darn you, open the tunnel!"

"OOOH!"

"Davey, what was that noise?"

"Nothing, Mama. Jeremy just threw his jar of baby food on the floor."

"DON'T TOUCH ANYTHING, DAVEY!
I'M COMING!"

"See, nothing happened, Mama."
"Well, there's no broken glass, anyway. I'll
ask the baby-sitter to clean this mess up."

"I'm glad you're wearing that dress to
school, Mama."

"Oh, do you like this dress, Davey?"

"No, but the carrots don't show too much."

"Oh, did I get carrots on it? I'll have to
change. Peel Jeremy a banana while I go
put on another dress."

"Look, Jeremy, I'm the daddy baboon, and you're the baby. Harrumph. Harrumph. Harrumph. Don't squeeze the banana, Jeremy. *Don't squeeze it, you big baboon!*"

"*Davey, don't call your little brother names!*"

"*He squeezed the banana!*"

"That's no reason to yell at him, dear.
You used to squeeze bananas, too, when
you were a baby."

"He isn't eating it, Mama."

"Maybe he'd like some milk with it.
Did you give him some milk?"

"No, Mama."

"Pour him half a cup of milk in his
Snoopy cup."

"Okay."

"Mama?"

"What is it now, Davey?"

"His Snoopy cup has green goop in it."

"Well, just use any plastic cup you can find."

"Look, Jeremy, I'm Harold, the ice-cream store man. I'm making a malted, la-lah, la-lah. Here you go-o-o-o-o-o-O-O-OH!"

"MAMA! JEREMY'S NOT HUNGRY,
AND I WON'T FEED HIM ANYMORE!"

"All right, all right. You don't need to have
a temper tantrum. Just let him crawl around on
the floor until I get there."

"Okay, Mama....Mama?"

"For heaven's sake, Davey, what is it this time?"

"You don't have to hurry, Mama. He isn't crying anymore."

"Jeremy's feeding himself."